MW00612914

BURN
With Me

A With Me IN SEATTLE NOVELLA

Burn With Me
Copyright © 2018 by Kristen Proby
All Rights Reserved.

This book may not be reproduced, scanned, or distributed in any printed
or electronic form without permission from the author. Please do not participate in or encourage piracy of copyrighted materials in violation of the
author's rights. All characters and storylines are the property of the author
and your support and respect is appreciated. The characters and events
portrayed in this book are fictitious. Any similarity to real persons, living or
dead, is coincidental and not intended by the author.

Cover Art:
Kari March Designs

Interior Design & Formatting::
Christine Borgford, Type A Formatting

Previously released under the title *Playing With Fire* in the anthology
Some Like It Hot 2014.

BOOKS BY
KRISTEN PROBY

The With Me in Seattle Series:
Come Away With Me
Under the Mistletoe With Me
Fight With Me
Play With Me
Rock With Me
Tied With Me
Breathe With Me
Forever With Me

The Love Under the Big Sky Series:
Loving Cara
Seducing Lauren
Falling for Jillian
Saving Grace

From 1001 Dark Nights:
Easy With You
Easy for Keeps

The Romancing Manhattan Series:
All the Way

BURN With Me

A With Me IN SEATTLE NOVELLA

NEW YORK TIMES BESTSELLING AUTHOR
KRISTEN PROBY

ONE
BAILEY

"Bailey! Can you help over here?" A harried volunteer with wide, nervous eyes yells for me as she has three out of breath firefighters standing before her.

"Of course," I reply and toss my clipboard on the floor, and begin to strip the closest firefighter to me.

My job doesn't suck.

Today is the annual Seattle Firefighter Stairclimb. Men and woman come from all over the country to participate in climbing a seventy-four-story building in downtown Seattle. They have to wear all of their gear, as much as an extra eighty pounds, up all seventy-four flights.

By the time they reach us at the top they are overheated and have to shed their gear as quickly as possible. That's where my volunteers come in.

"Get his helmet off, Molly. Yep, just like that."

The man before me is panting, can't talk, and sweating bullets.

He's also visually stunning.

"Okay, here's some water. Congratulations." I smile and guide the half-naked man to the rest area where others are drinking water, stretching and coming down from the high of climbing over thirteen hundred stairs.

I can't even imagine.

I've helped organize this event for three years in a row now. The charity benefits are large, which gets my own blood flowing. Stripping firefighters out of their gear doesn't hurt my feelings either.

I hurry back to the stripping area and continue helping the volunteers with the heavy gear.

"Bailey, can you help me with this?" Molly is struggling with an oxygen tank that's stuck on a coat, so I rush over and help her with it then pull the helmet off the out of breath man and feel my gut clench just as it always does every time I see Kevin.

"Good job, Kevin." I smile at the handsome man as he grins down at me and nods his thanks. I push a bottle of water in his hand and lead him over to the rest area. He's naked from the waist up, wearing only his firefighter pants and his boots. His torso is gleaming in sweat, his defined abs heaving with every labored breath.

Dear God, what would he look like while having sex?

"You okay?" he asks roughly, his green eyes bright with humor. I close my mouth with a snap, embarrassed that I was caught ogling him.

"I'm great." I smile wide and pat Kevin's shoulder. "Is Gray here too?" The two men typically enter the race together.

"Yeah, I think he ran ahead of me." He swigs half the bottle of water in a few gulps and scans the area looking for his best friend.

"Well you did great, congratulations." I move to walk away, but he catches my arm in his hand, pulling me up short.

"Are you heading over to the pub after?"

"Oh." I shake my head and wrinkle nose. "No. I have plans later."

He narrows his eyes and cocks his head, still panting, his blonde hair a sweaty mess, and dear God I've rarely seen anything as sexy as he is.

Except his best friend, Gray, who is equally as sexy.

And that's the problem.

"You should come," he says.

"I don't think so." He releases my arm, but continues to watch me with those amused green eyes.

"Come on, you know you can't resist a bunch of drunk firefighters who just ran up all those stairs."

Oh, I can resist them all right. It's you and your best friend I have a hard time saying no to.

"Bailey!" Someone calls from the other side of the room.

"I'll think about it. I have to go." I wave and jog back to Molly's side to help her as the bulk of climbers begin to pour through the doors.

The next fifteen minutes are a flurry of helmets, masks, coats, oxygen tanks and excited firefighters. They're pumped and proud, as they should be. They just worked their asses off.

"Do it! Do it! Do it!" The chanting has begun to my right in the rest area. People are whooping and cheering and to my utter shock, about twenty men who just climbed seven hundred and eighty-eight vertical feet are now doing pushups.

Including Kevin, and right next to him, Gray. Where Kevin is blonde, Gray has jet-black hair and bright blue eyes and both men are currently shirtless and executing perfect push-ups, their arms and backs flexing with every smooth motion up and down.

Hello, incinerated panties. Is it even legal in the state of Washington to look like that? Because it's seriously impairing for me to watch.

When they finish, Gray collapses onto the floor and Kevin pushes back on his haunches, laughing and panting and coated in a fresh layer of sweat.

"How do they do it?" Molly asks beside me, the last of the men having been stripped down and cooling off.

"I think they're super-human," I reply with a laugh. "I'm in decent shape, and there's no way in hell that I could do it. Just the thought makes me nauseous."

"Right?" She giggles and chews her thumbnail. "They're hot."

"Of course they are, they just climbed seventy-four floors."

She rolls her eyes at me. "Ha ha."

I smirk at the younger woman. "Yeah, they're hot."

"Are you coming to the pub after?" she asks.

"No." I shake my head and consult my clipboard blindly. At this point, everything on my list is done.

"You have to! Bailey, you helped *organize* this thing. You have to come celebrate."

I shrug a shoulder and bite my lip. I'd planned to go until Kevin asked if I'd be there. They have both asked me out and flirted relentlessly. They're handsome and sweet, although very different in personality. But they're best friends, and how does a girl choose between them?

She doesn't. She steers clear, that's what she does.

"One shot," Molly says with a hand over her heart. "We

will do one shot in celebration and then you can leave if you want. You've earned it."

I glance back over to where Kevin and Gray are talking and laughing with the others and feel my heart speed up. "One shot."

"Yes! I knew I'd talk you into it." She jumps next to me and then throws her arms around me, hugging me against her ample bust line.

"One shot," I repeat.

"If you say so."

GRAY

The pub is bursting at the seems with joyful firefighters, laughing and yelling, drinking and cat-calling.

It's completely typical after the stairclimb event.

"Here's your beer," Kevin says as he hands me the long-neck and taps the neck of his bottle to mine. "Good job, brother."

"Back at you."

"My time fell about twenty seconds this year." He winces and then shrugs.

I smirk and watch my friend as he scans the room, looking for Bailey I'm sure. We've both been looking for her. "I haven't seen her."

"She said she had plans tonight." His eyes meet mine and I can read him as if the thoughts were my own.

She's going to let another bastard put his hands on her.

"She has a life." I try to shrug off my own frustration. Kevin and I have been enamored with Bailey since the first time we met her at a BDSM event she attended last year. We've approached her separately but she's turned us down.

I can't figure her out. I don't know how deep into the BDSM community she is. She doesn't attend the club, Temptation, that Kevin and I both belong to. I know she's good friends with Matt Montgomery's girlfriend, but that's all I know.

And I want to know a hell of a lot more.

Suddenly the hairs on the back of my neck stand on end. My eyes search the crowd, and land right on her as she swigs back a shot and high-fives the volunteer she's been hanging out with all afternoon.

"Looks like she's had a change of heart," I murmur to Kevin and point her out to him, but his eyes are already pinned on her, bright green, and filled with lust.

I've seen the look on him many, many times over the years. We've shared women for years. I know what he looks like when a woman turns him on.

But I've never seen possessiveness mix in with the lust.

Not until this woman.

"She's interested," Kevin says with a half smile. "I caught her looking at us a few times today, and although her mouth said no when I asked her if she was coming here this evening, her body said hell yes when I touched her."

"You touched her?" My head whips around in surprise.

"Just her arm." He shrugs. "Like I said, she's interested."

"She'll come around." Kevin is a take control kind of guy. When an opportunity he wants doesn't immediately present itself to him, he makes it happen. I don't want him to move too quickly with Bailey and scare her off for good.

"When? When we're seventy? I'm fucking sick of waiting."

We both watch as two firefighters approach Bailey and her friend, flirting, offering to buy them drinks. The girls grin and nod, and I feel my blood boil when one of the guys wraps his arm around her shoulders and smiles charmingly down at her.

"Fuck," I whisper.

"I'm done waiting." Kev sets his beer on the table and stands. "She's not coming to us, and those assholes are coming on to her. You can wait until you're seventy if you want, but I won't."

And with that, he takes off through the crowd.

Fuck. I grab my beer and follow him. The crowd is thinning as some of the guys have headed home, or to another bar. Bailey's friend is laughing with the man who approached her, twirling her hair on her finger, giving off all the signals that if the guy plays his cards right, he'll be getting very lucky.

I watch with amusement as Kevin approaches Bailey from the side and rests a possessive hand on her shoulder while glaring at the other man who quickly backs away. She whirls around and turns her surprised gaze up to Kev.

"Hey, gorgeous," he murmurs with a smile. "What can I get you to drink?" He flags down the bartender as she shakes her head no, but licks her lips and glances at his chest, which is covered with a tight-fitting T-shirt.

Her friend vacates the stool next to her as she leaves with the guy who's about to get lucky, so I snatch it quickly and grin at my friend then at Bailey who as turned those big baby blues over to me.

"It's good to see you, Bailey."

"Hi Gray." She grins and offers me her hand, which I gladly take, but instead of settling for a simple handshake, I pull her hand to my lips and gently kiss her knuckles. Her eyes dilate as she watches and her mouth opens as her little pink tongue darts out to moisten her bottom lip, and it's like a punch to the gut.

Fuck, she's beautiful.

"You did a great job today," I say and keep her hand in mine.

"You guys did all the hard work," she insists. Kevin brushes her hair off her shoulder, and pulls his knuckle down the soft skin of her neck.

"You worked your cute little butt off," Kevin replies with a smile. "I know, I was watching." He winks and we both watch in fascination as her cheeks redden in embarrassment.

Interesting. She's shy.

The bartender sets fresh beers before Kevin and me and a pink fruity looking drink for Bailey. She immediately reaches for her drink and takes a very unlady-like swallow, making me grin. Kevin and I share an amused glance.

We'll get a drink or two in her to loosen her up a bit. Not enough to get her lit, just enough to relax her and bring her out of her shell a bit.

By her second drink, Bailey has relaxed quite a bit, laughing at our jokes, and chatting away about today.

"You guys did great," she insists. "I saw the final numbers. How do you stay in such good shape?"

"It's the job," Kevin replies. "It's hard work. Keeps us in shape."

"Some of us have to work harder than others," I add. Kevin is naturally fit and lean, while I have to work out every day to stay in this shape.

"Well, whatever you're doing, it's working for you," she replies and then slaps her hand over her mouth in mortification. I grin and take a sip of my beer. Kev's right, she's interested.

Maybe this won't be as difficult as we thought.

"We carry a lot of equipment," Kev continues, and I can see by the humor in his eyes that he has a plan up his sleeve. "Hoses, gear, people." He loops his arms under her legs and back and lifts her off the stool, takes her spot and settles her on his lap facing me, so she sandwiched between us. Her arms are wrapped around his shoulders and she's laughing.

"You just haul people around," she says dryly.

"Haven't you heard? We carry damsels in distress out of burning buildings all the time." Kevin grins down at her then over at me. "Right?"

"Almost every day," I lie easily, playing the game, but Kevin isn't fooling her. She just laughs moves to stand but Kev tightens his hold on her, keeping her in place.

"You're fine right here," he says.

She glances uncertainly between us, then picks her drink up and downs the rest of it.

"Another?" Kevin asks.

"No," I reply before Bailey can open her mouth. I shake my head but keep my eyes on Bailey's bright blue ones. "I think she's had enough."

"You're right, I should probably go home." She opens her purse and digs around for a moment, but I grip her chin in my fingers and lean in, plant my lips over hers and kiss her long and slow, stealing the breath right out of her. She moans as the tension leaves her and she sags against Kevin. I feel him wrap his arms around her middle, anchoring her as she melts into the kiss, opening her mouth to me sweetly.

She tastes like strawberries and heaven. Before I get too carried away, I back slowly away and watch in fascination as her eyes flutter open and she stares at me with her jaw dropped.

As if she realizes what she just did, and that she might have offended Kevin, she glances back at him.

"I'm sorr . . ."

Before she can finish, Kev catches her chin in his palm and guides her lips to his, kissing her just as long and just as sweetly, making her moan into his lips.

My dick throbs behind the fly of my jeans as I link my fingers through hers and hold onto her as she rides out the kiss. At last, Kev backs away and smiles smugly down at her.

She glances back and forth between both of us, licks her lips and whispers, "Holy shit."

"I think it's time we took you home," I reply with a wide smile. "What do you think, Kev?"

"Past time," he agrees and stands with Bailey still safe in his arms. "Let's go."

TWO
KEVIN

Jesus Christ, she has a body made for fucking sin. I cradle Bailey in my lap in the back seat of Gray's SUV—there was no way in hell I was going to let go of her long enough for the ride home. My hands frame her gorgeous face, and I kiss the fuck out of her. I can't get enough of the taste of her, all fruity and sweet and *Bailey*.

She moans and shoves her fingers in my hair, holding on tight, and presses her perfect tits against my chest. I didn't think it was possible, but my cock just got harder.

I'm going to explode before we even get home.

She leans her forehead against mine, panting and pulls her fingers down my cheek.

"Gray?" She says.

"Yes, sweetheart."

"Are we there yet?"

I grin and kiss her sweet lips gently, brushing over them lightly, making her squirm in my lap. She loves to kiss, which is good because she's going to get kissed plenty.

"Almost," Gray replies with a smile in his voice.

"Hurry," she whispers making both Gray and me laugh. My chuckle turns into a groan when she wiggles her perfect ass over my groin, making me see stars.

"Hurry, Gray," I agree gruffly.

"We're here," he replies, his voice tight with lust as he shoves the SUV into park and opens the back door for us. I climb out and reach back in for her, lifting her and heading for the front door.

"I can walk you know," she says with a grin and reaches a hand out for Gray. He immediately takes it and kisses her palm, his blue eyes on hers.

"I'm sure you can, but I'm quite content with you right here, princess." Gray unlocks the door and rather than stop in the living room, I march up the stairs and to my room. This may be the only night she spends in here, but I have to have her scent in my bed.

I have to.

Gray pulls the blankets back as I plant my lips on her forehead and lay her gently in the middle of the bed, between us, fully dressed.

We're going to unwrap her like a fucking Christmas present.

As she settles onto the bed, she rolls toward Gray who's more than happy to wrap his arms around her and cover her lips with his, kissing her thoroughly. She sighs and hitches one leg over his hip, pressing closer to him while I push against her back, grinding my still-covered cock against her ass, sweep her hair out of the way and lay wet kisses along her soft neck.

She smells amazing.

She reaches back and holds onto my ass, pulling me even

tighter against her.

I need to taste her.

I kiss down her arm and gently ease her back from Gray. He continues to keep her mouth occupied while I shimmy her shoes and pants off and toss them on the floor. When I glance up, I see Gray pulling her top over her head and he throws it in the same general direction her pants went before diving back for another taste of her mouth.

I can't blame him. She's fucking delicious.

I pull my shirt over my head, then nudge my way between her legs and drag the tip of my nose over her panties, from the top of the elastic, down over her pubis to her clit and finally down into her folds, inhaling the musky scent of her lust.

Fuck, she's so wet her barely-there black panties are soaked through, so I hook my thumbs in the lace at her hips and pull them down her legs, then lick my lips as I glance up at Gray. He's turned her head to the side and sends me a satisfied glance before nibbling down her jawline to the sensitive skin beneath her ear, making her scissor her legs on either side of me.

"God, you're gorgeous, sweetheart." I part her lips with my thumbs and watch in fascination as she opens to me, her pussy glistening with her juices. "Your clit is already swollen."

Gray growls and traps her lips with his again as I lean in and lap at her with the flat of my tongue from her tiny entrance all the way up to the thin strip of short hair above her clit and back down again, burying my face in her pussy, my tongue inside her and fuck her with my mouth.

It's the best fucking thing I've ever experienced. She cries out and arches her back, but Gray quickly lays his spread hand over her lower stomach, keeping her in place as I go to town on her.

"You like that, sweetheart?" He whispers in her ear. "Oh, baby, look at that." Bailey's eyes find mine as she watches me eat her out, lapping at her folds and then pull gently on her clit.

"Oh my God," she groans.

"Does that feel good?" Gray asks her, nuzzling her ear. She nods frantically and moans long and low as I push two fingers inside her.

"You both still have too many clothes on," she says as she pants and grinds her hips against my face.

"There's no hurry," Gray whispers. "Enjoy what he's doing to you, Bailey. Feel it."

She bites her lip and continues to watch me.

"Wait until you taste her," I growl and slide my fingers out of her and up through her lips to her clit and back in again, making her gasp and clench around me. "Fuck, Gray she's so fucking tight."

"I bet she's sweet as honey," he says and kisses her neck.

"Sweeter," I reply and kiss my way up her body. Gray shed her bra at some point, so I settle in to worship her perfect, pink-tipped breasts. "Look how beautiful you are."

"You are stunning, sweetheart," Gray whispers and gently pushes her hair away from her face.

"Thank you," she murmurs. "I'd love to see more of you." She smiles and bites her lip as Gray leans back and pulls his shirt over his head. Her hands are all over us. She's exploring my chest and shoulders, scrubs her nails through my hair. Jesus, my cock can't get any harder than it is. I unzip my jeans to ease the pressure on my dick and the sound draws Bailey's attention.

"Take your pants off."

"You're not in charge here, princess," I reply and then laugh when she snarls at me. "Just a little eager, are you?"

BAILEY

Fucking-A I'm eager! Jesus, my body is on fire, humming with electricity everywhere. Having two sets of lips and hands on me is incredible. I've never experienced anything even close to it.

Not to mention, it's been too damn long since the last time I got laid.

I just nod and watch them both as they shed their pants and boxer briefs and then slide back on the bed. They're both beyond enthusiastic, yet different. Kevin moves almost urgently while Gray is more laid back, content to set up camp and take his time.

And the two of them working in tandem is fan-fucking-tastic.

Their bodies are incredible. They're both tall. Their muscles are defined *everywhere*. It's like looking at two works of art.

And they're both impressively aroused.

They lie on either side of me, and Kevin immediately kisses my lips while Gray's head lowers to tug on my nipple while his hand glides down my belly to my pussy, where he circles my clit with his middle finger, sending sparks of electricity shooting up my spine and my hips off the mattress.

"Oh God!" I cry against Kevin's lips. I feel both men grin against me and my stomach flutters with nerves as my nipples harden even more.

"So responsive," Gray whispers and blows on my wet nipple. I glide my hands down each of their stomachs until I find both of their cocks and explore their lengths, making them both groan in pleasure.

Gray's cock is thicker, but they're about the same length, smooth and hard as steel.

"I need someone inside me," I whimper. Kevin bites my lower lip and Gray bites my nipple, keeping me right at the precipice of pain and pleasure. "Oh God, please."

"Didn't I say," Kevin begins and nips his way down my jaw to my neck. "That you're not in charge?"

"But I *need* you," I whisper. I'm not whining, it's pure, honest lust.

"We're not ready quite yet, sweetheart," Gray replies and nibbles his way down my body. "I haven't tasted you yet."

"Oh God, you're both trying to kill me."

They both chuckle, making my stomach flutter again. Their voices are like pure honey, sliding over me along with their talented fingers.

Finally, Gray nudges between my legs, kisses my inner thigh and works his way up while Kevin kisses down my neck to my breast.

This is sexiness overload.

I grip their hair in each hand and hold on as they work together to bring me to the edge of reason. Their small groans and whispered words of affection are filtering through the ringing in my ears, and when Gray plunges a finger inside me and pulses his lips around my clit, I come undone, exploding under their hands.

"That's right, princess," Kevin whispers by my ear. "Come for us. Just like that."

Gray kisses up my belly and settles in beside me, lapping at my breast as Kevin reaches toward his nightstand. "I can't wait," Kevin growls and kneels between my legs.

"Can I put it on you?" I ask with a smile. "I want to touch you."

Kevin's handsome face splits into a soft smile. He takes my hand in his and links our fingers as he covers me with his hard body and kisses me long and slow, and I swear to God I'm sinking right into the mattress. These men know how to use their mouths.

Kevin pushes back and watches my face as I position the condom on the tip of his cock and roll it down his length then guide him to my opening and keep my eyes trained on his as he slips just the tip inside me and bites his lip.

"Oh fuck me," he whispers reverently.

"She is," Gray responds with a chuckle. I reach for his hand blindly. He links his fingers with mine and they're holding both my hands now as Kevin pushes all the way inside me and stills, breathing hard, his brow sweaty.

"She's fucking amazing," Kevin says and looks up at Gray. My pussy clenches around Kevin as I release Gray's hand and reach for his cock. If we're going to do this threesome thing, we're going to do it right.

"Holy shit," Gray hisses when I begin to jack him in long, smooth strokes and lean over to lick around the head of his cock, under the rim and down the ridge of the vein that runs beneath it to his balls. His hips begin to move in slow thrusts as I take him in my mouth and suck, working him with both my fist and my lips as Kevin moves inside me, and they are suddenly moving in tandem.

"Look at me, sweetheart," Gray murmurs, cupping my chin as he gazes down at me. His eyes are hot and happy as he watches his cock disappear in my mouth. He's gentle, careful not to choke me, and lets me set my own pace, but I'm moving with the same rhythm as Kevin, who is fucking me in earnest now, his hips bumping against mine in a fast staccato.

"Fuck, I'm not gonna last. She's too fucking tight," Kevin growls and grips my hips tightly. He's going to leave fingerprints there.

I can't wait to fucking see them.

"Me too, man," Gray says, watching me with hot blue eyes. His balls lift and tighten and I know he's seconds away from coming so I suck harder and push my fist down, bearing down on the base of his cock as I clamp my pussy around Kevin's dick and tilt my hips in the air, pulling him as deeply inside me as I possibly can.

Kevin plants his thumb on my clit, taking me over the ledge with them.

Both men cry out as they come. I continue to suck on Gray's cock, swallowing the salty come as he shoots it into my mouth, and I shiver beneath them both with my own incredible orgasm.

As I come to my senses, I feel both of them stroking me, everywhere, soothing me. Gray is lying on his side, facing me, with his lips near my ear, whispering to me.

"You're so beautiful, sweetheart. Incredible." I grin and glance up at Kevin, who's still inside me, running his hands up and down my thighs, along my lower belly and back to my thighs again, grazing my skin with his fingernails.

"You guys are good at this," I sigh. Kevin chuckles and pulls out, moves off the bed and Gray rolls me toward him, running his hand down my back to my ass.

"Are you okay?" he whispers.

"I'm great." I kiss the tip of his nose and grin when I feel the bed dip behind me as Kevin wraps himself around my back, kissing my shoulder. "Whose room are we in?"

"Mine," Kevin whispers against my ear, sending a delicious chill through me.

"But we're about to leave." Gray's eyes sober as he stares at me, and I suddenly feel foolish. Of course, why would I think we'd snuggle. I came here for a night of hot sex, and that's what they delivered, thank God, but I'm sure they can't wait to dump me back at my car.

"You're really over thinking this," Kevin growls against my shoulder. "I can hear the wheels turning in that gorgeous head of yours."

"We're not taking you home," Gray agrees and drags his fingertips down my cheek. Neither of them has stopped touching me and it's pure heaven.

"Where are we going?"

"Down the hall," Gray says

I raise a brow but Kevin plants one more kiss on my shoulder and they both roll away, Gray pulling me along with him.

"Come on," Kevin says, leading the way.

I didn't pay attention to the house when we got here, I was too anxious to move on to the sex part of the evening. And for good reason, obviously.

"That's my room," Gray says and points to another good-sized bedroom with a big bed and jeans on the floor.

"And this," Kevin says and opens a door at the end of the hall. "Is the master."

"You guys don't use the master suite?" I ask with a frown and follow Kevin inside, Gray pulling up the rear. It's sparsely furnished with only a king-sized bed and dresser. The bed is bare, with the tags still on the mattress. There is no art on the walls, and through the open doorway, I can see that the closet is empty.

"No, we don't. Well, not yet."

I turn and face them both and plant my hands on my hips. "Why?"

They look at each other and then back at me. Gray's clearly thinking about his answer carefully. I've already come to realize that he's the thinker of the pair, less likely to ride by the seat of his pants.

"We haven't had a reason to," Kevin says and wraps his arms around me, hugging me tight.

What in the hell is that supposed to mean?

"Okay . . ." I frown as I pull out of Kevin's embrace. Suddenly Gray lifts me over his shoulder, firefighter-style, and heads for the bathroom.

"You make the bed, Kev, Bailey and I will be in the shower."

"Join us!" I squeal and wave to a laughing Kevin as Gray carries me away. "How can you have any strength left after today?"

"Oh, sweetheart, I think you're going to learn that when it comes to you, I have plenty of stamina."

Holy shit.

THREE
BAILEY

"You don't have to dry my hair," I murmur and watch in the mirror as Gray wields the blow dryer, pulling his fingers rhythmically through my long blonde strands, watching the hair as it falls down my back. Rather than make the bed, Kevin followed us into the bathroom and the three of us had quite a lot of fun in their enormous shower. We're all squeaky clean and dry, thanks to them. Kevin is making the bed while Gray blows my hair dry.

"Indulge me," he replies with a soft smile, meeting my eyes in the mirror. It's not a hardship to watch him move, that's for sure. The man's body is something to look at.

"How often do you work out?" My eyes are pinned to his hip. He's turned so his side is facing the mirror. Watching him move is mesmerizing.

He grins softly and lowers his lips to my ear. "Every day," he whispers and kisses my cheek then gets back to work on my hair. "How about you?"

I raise an eyebrow and let my eyes roam over my own body

in the mirror. I'm naked, but comfortable with the hot air blowing on me. It's making me relaxed and sleepy after such a long day with the climb and the rigorous sex with two very enthusiastic men. I'm not in particularly good shape. I'm slender, but not firm. I don't work out on a regular basis.

"I don't remember the last time I worked out," I reply honestly and without embarrassment. "Who has time?"

He laughs and nods as he smooths his hand down my hair. "You're in great shape, Bailey."

"I'm not complaining. I could stand to get on a treadmill now and again, but I'm on my feet a lot for work, so it all comes out in the wash." I shrug and watch as he sets the dryer aside and wraps his arms around my waist from behind, his eyes locked with mine in the mirror.

"Are you tired?" he asks.

"Exhausted. You must be too."

He nods and kisses my hair. These men are forever touching and kissing me. I haven't had this much affection in . . . well, ever.

Just then my stomach growls loudly, making us laugh.

"I guess I'm hungry too."

"Then we'd better feed you. Come on." He takes my hand and leads me into the master bedroom where Kevin is just throwing pillows onto the freshly-made bed. "We need food."

"Thank God, I'm fucking starving." Kevin smiles at me and kisses my forehead.

"Can I pull on one of your shirts?" I ask.

"Why?" Kevin asks. "We like having you naked."

"It would be more comfortable to eat with something on," I reply.

"Of course." Gray pulls me behind him to his room. His room is a bit messier than Kevin's. He crosses to a dresser and pulls out a blue T-shirt with the fire station emblem on it.

"It's a little big," I say with a laugh after I've pulled it on. But it's comfortable and it smells like Gray. I pull it up to my nose and take in a deep breath. "Smells good."

"You look good in my shirt," he says softly and kisses my forehead. "Let's feed you."

Kevin and Gray's home is beautiful. "How long have you lived here?"

"About a year," Gray replies as he leads me downstairs. "We had it built."

"I love it." The living room is typical for two men, big TV, comfortable furniture. The kitchen, however, is amazing. "I love this kitchen."

The cabinets are honey blonde wood with redwood trim. The stainless steel appliances gleam and the dark granite is smooth and wide, with plenty of work space.

"Do you like to cook?" Kevin asks. He's already pulled food out of the fridge and is cracking eggs. "I hope omelets are okay."

"Sounds perfect," I reply as Gray nods and pours us all some juice. "Yes, I can cook. I used to cook with my grandmother all the time when I was a kid."

"How are you at omelets?" Kevin asks with a cocky grin.

"I make the best omelet in the world."

"Prove it." He backs away from the stove and Gray bends over in laughter.

"Don't fall for it! He's just trying to get out of cooking."

"I don't mind." I shrug and quickly finish cracking the eggs and set about the task. "They're actually easy. The trick is knowing when to fold them over. You don't want to do it too soon or it'll be runny and I hate raw eggs." I shudder at the thought and plate the first omelet and pass it to Gray.

"Hey! Why does he get the first one?"

"He blew my hair dry," I reply with a grin. Gray smiles proudly and takes a bite of his food and moans out loud.

"That's it. You're staying. This is amazing."

I giggle and flip the second omelet. "Told you."

I pass Kevin his food and watch as he takes a bite, chews and swallows then grips my neck in his hand and pulls me in for a long, hot kiss.

"You're ours. You're never leaving."

I laugh and pour more eggs in the skillet for my own omelet. "You guys are too easy."

"No, sweetheart, we aren't." Gray's face is serious as he chews.

I swallow hard and take the skillet off the heat, plate my food and hop up on the granite countertop to eat my food. Mm, it's not half-bad, if I do say so myself. I was hungrier than I realized and devour my eggs quickly.

"You were hungry," Kevin says with a chuckle.

"Oh God, so hungry," I agree with eggs and cheese crammed in my mouth. "You wore me out."

A look passes between them and they laugh. I know they went easy on me tonight. I can only imagine what they're capable of together, but I haven't had sex in a while and it was vigorous and exciting, but exhausting.

"You'll need the calories, princess," Kevin says with a wink and loads our dishes into the dishwasher.

"Well, it was fun, guys. Thanks." I smile and hop off the

counter. "If you'll just take me to my car, I'll head home."

Their heads both whip around to me. Kevin is scowling and Gray's eyes are feral.

"No," Kevin says. "We want you to stay."

"The night?" I ask in surprise. "Oh. Well, okay."

They look at each other again and Kevin looks like he's about to say something, but Gray shakes his head. In warning?

What the hell?

"Kevin did make the bed," Gray reminds me. "We planned to keep you here with us for the weekend, Bailey."

I blink quickly and look between them. They're watching me, waiting for me to decide. I'm having a great time with them. They're sexy as all get out, but they're also funny and sweet.

I'd be stupid to say no.

And I may be a lot of things, but stupid isn't one of them.

"Why now?" I ask aloud. "We've known each other for a while, why are you guys doing this now?"

"Because we're damn tired of waiting for you to come to us," Kevin answers immediately. "Please stay with us for a few days."

"I'd like that." I smile shyly as they grin back at me.

"Come on. Let's try out that new bed," Kevin says as he kisses my hand and leads me out of the kitchen.

"Oh, I'm . . ."

"To sleep, sweetheart," Gray says with a laugh. "We could all use some sleep."

I crawl into the middle of the bed and bite my lip as each of them joins me on either side. Kevin turns me away from him and spoons me from behind. Gray lies facing me, brushes my hair off my face and drags his fingers down my cheek.

"I'm so happy you're here, Bailey," Gray says as he leans in and kisses my lips softly.

Kevin presses his lips to my shoulder. "Get some sleep, princess," he whispers.

Gray's eyes never leave mine as I give in to my heavy eyelids. I can hear them both breathing, feel them both against me, and I've never felt safer in my life. How did I get here, with these two amazing men? I always knew my sexual appetites were . . . *different*, but I had no idea that I'd be drawn to two men. That I might already be falling in love with them, and that scares the hell out of me.

But, I'm too tired to contemplate it tonight. I sigh deeply and slip into an exhausted sleep.

It's still dark when I wake up. I'm not sure what woke me. A sound? Is someone trying to break into my apartment? I stay still and listen, and realize I'm being held by a very strong arm from behind.

Kevin.

I grin and glide my fingertips over Kevin's arm, then realize that I don't feel Gray. I reach out for him, but the bed is cool where he should be.

I open my eyes and scan the dark room, but he's not here. Did he get called out on a call?

Surely he would have woken us.

I slip out from under Kevin's arm and go in search of Gray.

As I reach the kitchen, I hear the click, click, click of balls on a pool table. I didn't see a pool table earlier. I follow the sound to an open doorway off the kitchen. There's stairs down to a finished basement where Gray is bent over a pool table, taking a shot as I walk into the room. His eyes find mine and he straightens slowly, watching me as I move slowly toward him. He clenches his teeth, a muscle in his jaw flexes. Is he mad?

"Are you okay?"

He nods and lays his cue on the table. He pulled on basket-ball shorts before he came downstairs, but he's still shirtless. His dark hair is messy, like he's pushed his fingers through it over and over again.

"Can't sleep?"

"No."

I tilt my head and watch as he clenches and unclenches his fists. His shorts are tenting as he grows hard and my eyes fly to his.

"Take that shirt off," he directs me, his voice deceptively calm. My heart speeds up and my stomach clenches as I cross my arms and catch the hem of the shirt in my hands and whip it up over my head then drop it to the floor.

"Fuck," he whispers as his eyes travel down my body. "Do you have any idea how beautiful you are?"

I close the gap between us and cup his face in my hand.

"Do you have any idea," I echo back to him as he presses his lips to my palm, "how beautiful *you* are?"

He yanks me against him, plants both hands on the globes of my ass and lifts me effortlessly into his arms, wrapping my legs around his waist, devouring me with his mouth. He lays me down on the table, my hips against the edge and drags his nose down my jaw to my ear.

"Tell me you're on birth control, sweetheart."

"I am," I reply breathlessly.

I feel him push his shorts down his thighs as his lips return to mine. His tongue is sliding over mine in long, smooth strokes, intoxicating me. God, he can fucking kiss.

The head of his cock is at my entrance, slipping through my slick folds.

"You're so fucking wet."

"You turn me on," I reply and gasp as he pushes inside me, buried balls-deep. "Oh my God."

"Kev was right, you're so fucking tight," he says through clenched teeth. "I can't go slow, Bailey. I'm so sorry, baby."

"Don't go slow." I shake my head against the table, lost in watching him try to reel in his control and failing horribly. It's empowering to know that I do this to him. He pushes my legs back against my chest and braces himself on the backs of my thighs as he begins to pound in and out of me, thrusting hard, so deep inside me I don't know where I end and he begins.

"So fucking amazing," he growls and I know he's close. He pushes me even farther into the table as he leans against me, holds himself inside and comes apart, grunting as he spills inside me, and as he rocks his pelvis against my clit, he pushes me over the edge with him.

Gasping for breath, he lifts me effortlessly into his arms and caries me, still inside me, to the small basement bathroom where he sets me on the vanity and leans his forehead against mine, his eyes closed, breathing me in.

"Amazing," he repeats before kissing my forehead and pulling out gently. He wets a washcloth and washes me clean, then himself and lifts me back into his arms.

"You two are forever carrying me around," I say with a grin. "What's up with that?"

"We like having you in our arms, sweetheart."

He turns out the lights, but instead of taking us upstairs to bed, he settles on one of the long, wide, soft couches and covers us with a blanket. I'm lying on him, as though he's my bed.

"Is this okay?" he asks as he wraps those magical arms around me and holds me close.

"I've never been more comfortable." I can feel him smile against my head as he presses a kiss there.

"Good."

"Why are you awake? You should be exhausted. Do I have to remind you of the thirteen-hundred stairs you climbed today?"

"No, my body is reminding me enough." He chuckles and drags his fingertips up and down my bare back under the blanket, sending shivers through me.

"Talk to me, Gray."

He sighs and for a moment I think he's going to refuse.

"I've had insomnia for years, Bailey. It seems to come with the job. Working so many different shifts, being up for long hours, affects some more than others. It's not a big deal."

"It's a big deal, Gray. Your body needs to rest."

"Hmm." His heart is slow and steady against my ear. I can't resist turning my head and pressing a soft kiss there, then nuzzling him with my cheek. "You're a sweet woman, Bailey."

FOUR
GRAY

"You're a quiet man, Gray."

I chuckle and brush the soft blonde hair off her shoulder. "First let me ask you this: how do you feel? About what the three of us did?"

She stills and I can hear the wheels turning in that beautiful head of hers.

"I had a good time," she replies truthfully.

"I'm glad. So did we."

"Really?" She sounds surprised, making me frown.

"Of course." I tilt her head back so I can look into her eyes. "Why wouldn't we?"

"I'm not naïve, Gray. I know you guys went easy on me."

Yes, sweet girl, we went easy on you. "There hasn't been anything easy about you, sweetheart."

"You know what I mean." She lowers her head back to my chest and tightens her arms around my torso, clinging to me. God, she feels amazing, like she was made to fit against me, just like this.

I sigh and lay my lips on her head, breathing in her clean scent. "As long as we all have fun, it's consensual and comfortable, respectful, who cares?"

She shrugs a shoulder, but I can tell she's still uncomfortable.

"Bailey, we enjoyed the hell out of you, and plan to do so again. There was nothing wrong with what we did."

"I don't feel like it was wrong," she replies quickly, making me smile. Fuck yes, she's perfect for us.

"Then what's bothering you?"

"I guess when I think of threesomes, it's a lot more . . ."

"Okay, let's get something straight," I interrupt quietly. "You're not a porn star or a hooker, Bailey, and we will never treat you that way. You're precious and we care about you. We want to enjoy you, and we want for you to enjoy us. That's all. So whatever form that takes when the three of us are together is exactly that: between the three of us. There are no preconceived notions about what it's supposed to look or feel like."

She sighs and kisses my chest again, making my dick stir. Jesus, all she has to do is breathe and I want her. Watching Kevin inside her as she sucked my cock was the best experience of my life. We've done dirtier, more erotic things with other women, but I can't even remember them now. All I can see is Bailey. And being inside her on that pool table was just like sliding home.

"I like that," she whispers.

"Good. But if you ever want to wear a sexy nurse costume with high heels and play doctor, I'm pretty sure we'll be into it."

"Of course," she replies dryly. "How long have you known Kevin?" she asks, changing the subject.

"For as long as I can remember. We were next door neighbors growing up."

"Oh, that's cool. Did you get into all kinds of trouble together?"

"You have no idea," I laugh as I think of us as young boys, running wild through the neighborhood.

"How long have you been . . ."

"Sharing women?" I finish for her and smile when she nods. "Since college. We dated normally through high school and even into college. Kevin had a girlfriend who wanted to try the threesome thing, so we did. We both knew that something felt like it was missing before, but we didn't know what until that experience."

"So you've always shared since then?" she asks softly.

"Usually. We have had sexual partners that we didn't share, but that's not often. Hell, we don't share often either."

"But you belong to the club," she says in confusion.

"I was wondering if you knew about that," I reply.

"People talk," she says and jerks her shoulder in a shrug.

"We do."

"So you're into BDSM too?"

"No, not really."

"Then why the club? You're both hot, you can't tell me that either of you have problems finding partners."

I love that she's so attracted to both of us, because God knows, we think she's the sexiest woman on the face of the earth.

"Kevin has a tendency to be an exhibitionist, and there are usually like-minded people at the club."

"Like minded as in threesomes or exhibitionists or both?"

"Both, I guess," I rub my hands up and down her slender back.

"Oh." I feel her frown against my chest, making me chuckle again.

"I'm more vanilla of the two of us."

"Neither of you are vanilla," she says with a smile in her sweet voice.

"I guess you're right. Tell me about you. What are your tastes?"

She sighs deeply, as if I've just asked her to cure cancer.

"I haven't ever been able to figure that out."

"What do you mean?"

"Sex has always just been . . . *okay.* For a long time I hoped I was submissive so I could fit into that category."

"There are no categories, sweetheart."

"You know what I mean."

"You're no submissive." I laugh at the thought of it. No, Bailey is no man's submissive.

"No way," she agrees with a chuckle. "But missionary sex is so boring. There has to be a happy medium, right?"

I give her a moment to process her thoughts, kissing her head and caressing her slender back.

"Is it weird that I like to be intimate with two men at once?" she wonders out loud.

"Clearly you're asking the wrong person that question, sweetheart." I snort and look down into laughing blue eyes. "I don't think it's weird at all."

"Of course you don't."

"Does it feel weird to you?"

"No." She frowns.

"What then?"

She looks like she's going to say something, but she shakes

her head and lays back down on me. "Nothing."

I sigh as sleep weighs my eyelids down. Finally. My body is singing from the climb yesterday and the long hours being awake. Bailey's breathing has evened out and I know she's gone back to sleep.

I kiss her head, thankful that she's here with us, and follow her into a dreamless slumber.

I wake to sunlight coming through the small windows of the basement and Bailey still sleeping soundly on my chest. I glance up to find Kevin leaning against the doorway, smiling smugly at us.

"I'm starting breakfast. No rush, man. Wake her up and enjoy her."

"Thanks," I whisper as he turns to leave. I brush the hair off Bailey's face and kiss her forehead. "Wake up, sweetheart."

"Mmmph," she replies, making me grin. God, she's adorable in the morning.

"Kevin's making us breakfast, sweetheart." She sighs and buries her face in my chest, takes a long, deep breath and wiggles against me, her small naked body moving against mine, making my hard cock even harder.

"You're so hard," she whispers.

"Every morning," I agree with a wicked smile.

"Not that," she laughs. "Well, yeah, that, but the rest of you too."

"Was I uncomfortable?" I kiss her forehead and turn us carefully to the side, making sure she doesn't fall.

"No, I haven't slept that well in a long time." She grins and kisses my chin. "Thanks for the talk. And the pool game."

"My favorite way to play pool." My smile fades as I watch her face.

"We didn't use protection," she whispers.

"Kev and I never go without protection, Bailey. Ever."

"I've got the birth control under, well, control." She smiles and buries her face in my chest again. "And I haven't been with anyone in a couple years."

"*Years?*" I ask in shock. Holy shit! *Years?* "How is that possible? You're gorgeous and smart and sexy as fuck."

She shrugs and hugs me tightly. "I just haven't met anyone who interested me."

"We are tested every year. We're clean, sweetheart."

"I wouldn't be here if I thought otherwise."

"Okay then." I sniff loudly, the smell of bacon filling my nose. "Let's go see what Kevin has cooking."

BAILEY

"This is where you live?" Kevin says with a scowl. They've just climbed out of Kevin's car behind me. We picked my car up and they followed me home so I could pack a few things for the rest of the weekend. I look up at the old apartment building and bite my lip with a shrug.

"Yeah."

Gray and Kevin share a look and cross their arms over their chests.

"What?" I ask in exasperation.

"This place is old, and it looks like it hasn't been updated since the day it was built."

"Which makes it cheap," I agree and roll my eyes as I turn and lead them up to my small apartment. They're right, I don't exactly live at the Ritz. But it's inexpensive and I'm hardly here anyway.

I lead them into my apartment and they both scan the inside.

"I don't like this neighborhood," Kevin says, his hands on his hips as Gray wanders through my space, looking under sinks and at my heating ducts.

"Then it's a good thing you don't live here," I reply sassily and bat my eyes at him before walking into the bedroom to pack a bag. "What are we doing today?"

"We're going out on the boat," Gray says absentmindedly as he examines my heater in the bedroom. "You shouldn't cover this vent with this desk."

"There's nowhere else to put the desk," I search through my dresser for the new black bikini I bought last year.

"This is a fire trap," Kevin calls from the other room. His voice is laced with disgust.

"It is not." I roll my eyes and shove some jeans and a T-shirt into my bag. "It's just old."

"I'm the expert, princess," Kevin says as he pokes his head around the doorjamb. "Trust me, this is a fire waiting to happen."

"What do you want me to do?"

"Move out of it," Gray responds immediately, making me laugh.

"Right. That's easy to do. This is what I can afford."

"I know who your parents are," Kevin says from the doorway where he's leaning his shoulder, his arms crossed over his chest.

"Yeah, so does most of the state of Washington."

"How does a senator's daughter live here?"

"The senator and his wife want very little to do with their daughter," I reply honestly, my voice void of emotion. "It's been that way since said daughter decided to flip off her law degree and organize charity events for a living. Such a disappointment. I don't need their fucking money. I am not cold or hungry. I don't need designer labels in my closet, guys. I'd rather donate the money to someone else who *is* cold and hungry."

Kevin advances on me and pulls me into his arms for a big hug as Gray swears under his breath.

"Your parents are idiots," Kevin whispers into my ear.

"On that we can agree." I smile and shrug. "This is old news to me guys, so if you expect me to fall apart and cry delicately because my daddy refuses to buy me a designer handbag, you're going to be disappointed."

"Strong girl," Gray says and kisses my head as Kevin continues to hold me close. "Finish gathering your things so we can go enjoy the boat."

"What kind of boat do you have?" I'm thankful for the change of subject, but I can tell by the look that passes between the guys that it won't be over forever.

"A sporty one that goes fast," Kevin replies with a smile as he moves away from me so I can finish packing my bag.

KEVIN

It's the perfect day to be out on the boat. We launch her into the water and set out fast on the blue water of the sound, bouncing off the waves made by the ferries.

"Woohoo!" Bailey cries with a wide smile and high-fives Gray, who's sitting next to her, his arm wrapped around her shoulders. I love seeing them together. I love that she's so comfortable with both of us after such a short time.

Because I wasn't lying when I said she's ours and she's never leaving. Bailey may think we were joking, but we couldn't be more serious.

She won't be returning to that death trap of an apartment. Just the thought of that place makes my blood boil. She's lucky it hasn't burned down around her as it is.

Damn stubborn woman.

"Wanna drive?" I call out to her. Bailey's smile returns full-force, hitting me like a punch in the gut. God, she's fucking beautiful.

She stands and hurries over to me and I tuck her between me and the wheel. She wiggles that barely-covered ass against my growing cock, making me want to bend her over and fuck the hell out of her right here.

"Behave," I growl in her ear, making her laugh.

"How do I do this?" She asks excitedly, looking out over the water. "It's so pretty out here!"

"Have you ever been on a boat before?" Gray asks from his seat, watching us both.

"Nope." She shakes her head. "Mom was always afraid of water. Her brother drown when they were children."

"That's sad," I mutter and position her hands on the wheel, keeping mine over them. God, her hands are so small. "Just keep her steady. Keep an eye on the boats around us, careful not to get to close to any of them, and take us wherever you want to go."

"This is so fun!" She exclaims. "How do we go faster?"

"Oh God, she's a speed demon," Gray says with a laugh.

"My kind of girl," I reply with a grin. "Here's the throttle." She pushes the throttle, sending us speeding over the water. "Whoa! Not that fast."

She laughs and kisses me fast and hard then turns back to her task at hand, driving the boat through the blue water. There's not a cloud in the sky today, and out here on the water it's cool and perfect.

Perfect with the two people I care about the most.

"Where should we go?" She swipes at a strand of hair that's escaped her ponytail.

"We can head north and you can see some pretty impressive houses," I suggest. "Or, we can go around the islands and maybe see some wildlife."

"Oh, let's go around the islands!" She claps her hands when I pull mine off hers.

"Hands on the wheel, princess."

With her driving on her own now, I rest my hands on either side of the wheel and lean into her, burying my face in her neck. Fuck, she smells of clean air and soap and I can't get enough of her. I nibble her soft skin, then catch her earlobe between my lips and suck softly.

"I can't concentrate when you do that," she warns me, but she leans into me when I press my cock against her ass.

"I'm going to bury myself inside you tonight," I whisper in her ear. Goosebumps break out over her skin. I grin and press a kiss to that sensitive skin under her ear. "I'm going to make love to you until you can't remember your own name."

"Well that sounds like fun," she replies and glances up at me with bright, lust-filled eyes, then glances nervously over at Gray. He catches my gaze, and I nod. I take the throttle and slow us down to a stop, content to let us drift while we talk to our girl.

"Bailey, I know that you and Gray made love in the basement last night." Her cheeks pinken and she bites her lip. "And that's awesome. There will be times that we will have you to ourselves. And other times we'll have you together. There's no need for you to feel guilty that you enjoy having sex with each of us separately."

"I don't want to make either of you jealous because I am attracted to you both and I enjoy being with both of you," she admits with a shrug. "I don't want it to get weird."

"It's not weird because we're not jealous," Gray says and takes her hand in his, kissing her palm. "Remember what I said last night, sweetheart. It's what we decide between the three of us. It's our relationship, no one else's."

"Relationship?" she asks in surprise.

"Do you think we bring women out on our boat often? Ask them to stay the weekend?"

"I have no idea," she replies with a frown.

"We don't," I reply and tip her face up with my finger. "We don't."

She looks back and forth between us and then laughs ruefully. "Okay. I guess we'll figure it out as we go."

"That's the plan." Gray kisses her forehead and then her lips, then passes her off to me and I do the same. "My turn to drive," he says with a wolfish grin. "Let's see how fast this fucker can go."

"Alright!" Bailey exclaims in excitement. Oh yeah, she's perfect for us.

FIVE
BAILEY

"That was delicious." Gray sits back in his seat on the patio and pats his flat belly. "You weren't kidding when you said you love to cook."

I smile proudly and sip my wine. "Thank you, but all I did was throw a few steaks on the grill and toss a salad."

"That's heaven to us, princess," Kevin says with a wink. These guys are so . . . *amazing*. What's the catch here? They're sweet. All day on the boat they made sure my sunscreen was fresh. They brought me diet sodas. Gray pulled my feet in his lap and rubbed them while Kevin drove us back to shore. They're the most affectionate, attentive men I've ever met.

A girl could get used to this, and that's something that scares me. This is a weekend fling. I'll go home tomorrow and back to my normal life. I guess we could continue a sexual relationship now and then, but their work is demanding, and so is mine. I have no idea how our schedules would mesh.

"You're thinking awfully hard over there," Gray murmurs and sips his water.

"What's on your mind?" Kevin asks.

I'm not going to tell them that I'm not sure how our schedules are going to mesh for casual fucking. Not in this lifetime.

"I was just thinking about the strawberry shortcake I'm about to whip together," I lie easily and smile at the men. Gray narrows his eyes on me and he looks like he's about to say something when his cell phone rings on the table at his elbow.

Saved by the bell.

"McDermitt." He doesn't take his eyes off me as he listens to the voice on the other end of the line. "Give me ten." He ends the call and stands, rounds the table to me and pulls me out of my chair. He covers my mouth with his and kisses me firmly before pulling back and cradling my face in his hands. "This conversation isn't over, sweetheart. I have to go to work for a while."

"What's up?" Kevin asks.

"Multiple car accident," Gray responds with a sigh.

"How bad is it?" I ask.

"I have no idea," Gray replies. "Won't know until I get there."

"Be safe." I wrap my arms around him and hug him close.

"I'll be fine." He kisses my forehead, waves at Kevin and takes off through the house.

"It's already pretty late," I comment. We didn't come off the water until dusk, and now it's dark. "Does this happen very often?"

"Sometimes, yeah. We get called in at a moment's notice, even on our days off."

I nod and begin clearing dishes, carrying them to the kitchen. Kevin joins in and before long the patio table is cleared off and cleaned and we have the dishwasher loaded and the kitchen clean, too.

I've just finished wiping down the countertops when I feel Kevin move up behind me and wrap his arms around my middle and bury his face in my neck.

"Hey you," I whisper.

"Hey beautiful," he responds. "I think you've done enough work for the day." He takes the dishrag from my hands and tosses it into the sink then turns me in his arms and pulls me against him. "What can I do for you, Miss Whitworth?"

"I don't need anything," I reply honestly and brace my hands on his chest as I look up into his kind, happy face. His blonde hair is still wind-blown and his green eyes are smiling down at me sweetly. I nuzzle his chin with my nose, then place a kiss there. "Although, I could use a shower."

"I think that's the best idea you've had all day," he says with a grin and kisses my forehead before leading me up the stairs to the master bedroom. I love this room. The bed is super comfortable and the room is big, with plenty of floor space to add a chair and ottoman to use as a reading nook. I can picture pretty paintings on the walls, and all of our clothes mingling on the floor and in the closet.

Keep dreaming, sister.

Kevin leads me into the spacious bathroom and starts the shower, then turns back to me and pulls my swimsuit cover-up over my head. "You looked gorgeous today," he says softly.

I smile as I hook my finger in the waistband of his swim shorts and tug him closer to me. "So did you." His stomach muscles flex beneath my finger as I run it back and forth over the smooth flesh. "But I think you'll look even better when we shed these shorts."

"Yeah? Let's find out." He winks and pulls the shorts down his legs and kicks them aside. "Better?"

I lick my lips as I stare at his hard cock, firm legs and numerous abs. "Oh yeah. Much better."

"You're a naughty girl, Bailey," he murmurs and tugs the strings holding my bikini together. The scraps of fabric fall away and we're left standing in the bathroom, facing each other, naked. "Mm, I think I prefer you this way too."

I reach up and cup his cheek in my hand, then pull my fingertips down his face, his neck, and lower, down his chest and abdomen and finally find his cock.

"I haven't tasted you yet," I say softly. His cock twitches in my hand as Kevin growls low in his throat. "Do you mind?"

"Do I mind?" He laughs and tucks a strand of my hair behind my ear. "Baby, that's like asking me if I mind if you breathe. You can do any damn thing you want to me and I'll fucking love it."

I tilt my head to the side and watch his face as I pump up and down the length of him, reveling in the velvety feel of his cock. The room is filling with steam as I lower myself to my knees and circle the head with my tongue.

"I love that little tongue of yours," he growls roughly and grips my hair in his fist as I sink over him, taking him all the way to the back of my mouth and swallow around him, massaging the tip. "Fuck me."

KEVIN

She's trying to kill me. Her perfect mouth is wrapped around my cock and I see stars as she pulls up, those lips squeezing me. Too much more of this and I'll come in her mouth, and I don't want to do that.

I want to come inside her.

"Bailey," I begin but break off on a sob when she cups my balls and kneads them roughly. Jesus Christ, my spine is tingling. "Baby, you have to stop."

She shakes her head no and increases the pace with her mouth and fist. Before this is over before it really begins, I reach down and pull her to her feet then lift her in my arms and march toward the shower.

"I wasn't done," she pouts. I kiss her sweet lips and chuckle.

"Sweetheart, I was about to be done, and I have plans for you." Her blue eyes brighten at that. I set her on her feet under the hot spray of water and get to work washing her. Every delectable inch of her is covered in soap before I rinse her and get to work on her hair, washing the thick locks.

"You have such great hands," she moans. Her eyes are closed and she's leaning into my hands. "God, you can just rub me all the time."

"That's the plan, princess," I murmur and kiss her lips, then rinse her hair and the rest of her soapy body. Before I can pull her out of the shower, she grabs the soap and returns the favor, washing me from head to toe.

I'm so fucking turned on, it's a wonder my dick hasn't spontaneously combusted.

When I'm clean, Bailey drops the washrag on the floor and jumps back in my arms. I catch her against me easily, spin, and pin her against the tile wall, kissing her savagely.

"Fuck, I need you now."

"Take me now, damn it." She grips my hair in her fists and pulls my face back to hers and kisses me crazy. I guide myself inside her and have to still in fear of coming on impact.

"Jesus Christ, you're so fucking tight, Bailey." She grins against me and bites my lower lip as she tilts her hips, dragging me further inside her. "God damn, baby."

"You feel so good," she whimpers and I can't stand it anymore, I begin moving hard and fast, fucking her against the wall like I'm a man possessed. She bounces roughly with every thrust. Her jaw is dropped, her bright blue gaze pinned to mine as I make her mine.

"I love this; fucking you, feeling you," I turn and flip off the water and carry her to the bed, not bothering to dry us off. I can't stop being inside her.

I can't stop.

I climb on the bed with her, grip her hands in mine and guide them over her head, holding her there as I continue to thrust in and out in a fast, hard rhythm.

"Oh my God," she says and moans. "Kevin, it's so good. So damn good."

"Fuck yes, it's good." I pin both of her hands in one of mine and slide the other down her arm to her face. I cup her chin in my palm, plant my fingers on one cheek and my thumb on the other and kiss her with all I have. Jesus, I don't know where I end with her. I open my eyes to find her watching me, her hips meeting me with every jerk of my hips, and I know, in this moment, I'm in love with her.

The orgasm starts low in my back and works its way into my cock. I push in and grind against her clit and she bites my lower lip.

"Please let my arms go. I want to hold you when you come."
Her eyes are pleading. Fuck, how can I ever say no to her? I
release her and she clings to me as we both fall over the edge,
watching each other with wide eyes as the shivers take over
and pull us under.

GRAY

Spending the past five hours consoling a heartbroken widow
is the absolute worst part of my job. I hate it. It made my
heart hurt to watch her grief, and inspired this urgent need to
get back home to Kev and Bailey, to see that they're safe and
whole and *mine*.

I let myself into our dark house and listen for any sexy
sounds coming from upstairs, hoping I can join them, but the
house is still. They must be asleep.

That's fine too. It's usually difficult for me to find sleep on
a normal day, and impossible when I've had a fatality to deal
with, but I'll happily climb into that bed and hold Bailey all
night long if she'll let me.

I climb the stairs and bypass my bedroom for the master.
Sure enough, Kev and Bailey are cuddled up, sleeping. He's
spooning her, his nose buried in her hair and his arm wrapped
tightly around her middle, even in sleep.

I decide to take a quick shower, washing off the salt from
our ride on the water today, and the sadness from work.

When I return to the bed, they haven't moved. I slide between the sheets and lay my head on Bailey's pillow, just inches
away from her. I brush her hair off her face and tuck it behind

her ear then gently skim my knuckles down her cheek.

God, I'm so in love with her I can hardly breathe. I hope Kevin is on board with this because she's ours. She's not going back to that firetrap of an apartment.

I slide the pad of my thumb over her lower lip and grin when she gently kisses it and opens her sleepy eyes to smile at me softly.

"Hey," she whispers.

"Go back to sleep, sweetheart."

She snuggles down further in the bed, but continues to watch me quietly. Her hands are moving back and forth over the length of Kevin's forearm, her fingertips grazing over his skin and my own skin prickles at the thought of having her hands on me. Her touch is addictive.

Finally, she leans forward and lays her soft lips on mine, kissing me sweetly, and then leans back and smiles, looking me in the eyes.

"We missed you tonight," she whispers.

Best fucking words I've ever heard.

"I missed you too."

"Are you okay?"

I nod silently and brush at her hair again, although there's none to move off her face. I just can't stop touching her.

"Was it bad?" she asks softly.

I just nod again and sigh. I know my eyes are sad. I've never been good at hiding my emotions and right now I'm too exhausted to try.

"I'm sorry." She kisses me again, then wraps her arm around my waist, pulling me fully against her, so Kevin is pressed to her back and I'm pressed to her front. "Will you sleep?"

"I'll try." Her lips tip up as she nods once.

"Sleep, babe. For me."

Babe. Yep, completely in love with her.

"Okay."

She drifts back to sleep with her hand resting on my ass, her breaths low and even. Kevin's breaths match hers, and my eyes suddenly feel heavy with fatigue and exhaustion and for the first time in as long as I can remember, I drift into sleep easily.

SIX
KEVIN

"Is she still asleep?" I ask as Gray comes into the kitchen. He's pulled on sweats, and yawns widely as he scratches his head.

"Yeah, still out."

"What time did you get home? I didn't hear you." I flip the French toast and check the bacon in the oven.

"It was pretty late. You guys were sacked out." He pours himself a cup of coffee and sits on a stool at the breakfast bar. "We need to talk."

"So talk," I reply and whip up some eggs to scramble.

"I'm in love with her," he says quietly. I set the bowl on the counter, turn to face my friend and tilt my head as I study him.

"So we're on the same page there," I reply and lean my hands on the countertop. "Unless you're telling me you want her for yourself."

"What the fuck? Of course not." He shakes his head and takes another sip of coffee and my stomach muscles loosen. "I want to make sure that you feel the same way because the way I see it, she's staying."

"Oh yeah." I wave him off and pour the eggs into the skillet. "She's definitely staying. It's better with her than either of us ever hoped for, man."

"She's everything," he replies, staring down into his mug. "All I could think about was getting home to the two of you last night. Fuck, we built this house for her and we didn't even know it."

I nod as I plate our breakfast and load up two trays to take to the bedroom.

"So," I say and lean my hip against the counter. "Now we have to convince her that this is where she needs to be."

"I don't think it's going to be difficult." Gray shrugs arrogantly. He's always been a little arrogant.

"She's known us for two days, man."

"She's known us for over a year," he argues, his eyes cold and stubborn.

"In passing, yes, but she's only known us intimately for two fucking days."

"Does it feel like two days?" he demands.

I shake my head and laugh. "Bailey is logical and that logical brain of hers is going to tell her it's too soon."

Gray stands and grabs a tray. "Let's go spend the day with her and talk about it tonight."

BAILEY

"Wake up, princess." Kevin's voice is in my ear and it feels like fifty hands are running up and down my body in the most delicious ways.

"If I'm dreaming, don't wake me up," I mumble against the

pillow. Both of my men chuckle softly but continue to stroke my flesh, kneading my muscles. "Dear God, waking up to a massage? Are you kidding me?"

I turn onto my back and grin up at the guys who are kneeling at either side of me.

"Good morning," I say with a smile.

"Good morning, sweetheart," Gray says as he leans down to kiss me softly. He smells of coffee.

"Can I have some coffee?" I ask against his lips. His blue eyes are happy as he nuzzles my nose with his, then backs away and gestures to two trays sitting at the end of the bed.

"You can have whatever you want," Kevin replies. "I made breakfast."

"Holy crap, that looks like a buffet," I reply and stare at the steaming food. My belly rumbles and I smile ruefully. "And I'm hungry."

Gray fills a plate with a little of everything and passes it to me along with a cup of coffee. Soon, we're all sitting cross-legged on the bed, eating the delicious feast and chatting as if we've been friends for years.

"We thought we'd just lay low today," Kevin says as he munches on a slice of crispy bacon. "It's raining, so we can watch movies or read or play pool. Whatever you want."

I lower my fork to my plate and cringe. "I usually meet up with my friend Nic on Sundays for appetizers and wine."

They exchange a look before Gray responds. "Would you mind cancelling just this once? We normally wouldn't ask you to, sweetheart, but well, we're not ready to end the weekend yet."

"We'll remember for future reference that your Sunday afternoons are booked," Kevin agrees immediately and they're both staring at me with so much hope in their eyes, how can I resist them?

"Sure, I'll text her." I shrug one shoulder and finish my breakfast. "I'll clean this up."

"No, you won't," Gray says, taking my plate from me.

"But Kevin cooked. I can clean up."

"Nope. We'll put the dishes in the sink for later and go down to the basement to play." Kevin holds one of his T-shirts out for me to slip into. The guys are both in sweatpants and T-shirts.

"Can I wear pants too? I brought some."

"No," they reply in unison, making me laugh.

"We like having access to you," Kevin says with wink before leading me downstairs to the basement. Gray is behind us with the trays, drops them off in the kitchen and joins us by the pool table.

"Gray and I had some fun down here the other night," I mutter as I stare at the pool table, the events from Friday night playing in my head.

"Really," Kevin replies with a naughty grin. "We'll most likely have some fun down here again today. I doubt we'll be able to keep our hands off of you."

Gray comes up behind me and slides his hands up my thighs, under Kevin's shirt to cup my ass then travel around to my belly. It takes me a moment to realize that the moaning in the room is coming from me. Good God his hands are like heaven.

"That feels good," I whisper. "Let's skip pool and go straight to the fun stuff."

"You're not in charge," Gray whispers in my ear before biting my lobe, sending shivers down my spine.

"When do I get to be in charge?" I ask.

"You don't," Kevin replies.

This is why I love them. When I'm with them, I don't have any worries. My mind can calm and I don't have to worry about anything, overthink anything. I just have to feel. And oh, God, what they make me feel!

"Can't you at least take your shirts off?" I ask.

"We could place a bet," Gray suggests as he releases me into Kevin's arms. Kevin hugs me close and kisses my head as Gray racks the balls.

"What kind of bet?" I ask and watch the way his arms flex as he shuffles the balls in the plastic triangle.

"If you win, we'll take our shirts off."

"I like this idea," I reply with a smile and kiss Kevin's chest through his shirt. "You smell good."

"Do you want to know what we get if *we* win?" Kevin asks with a laugh.

"No because you're not going to win," I reply as I pull out of his arms and choose a cue.

Gray's eyebrows have climbed into his hairline as he watches me circle the table. "We play almost every day."

I shrug as though it doesn't matter and smile sweetly. "Okay, what do you get in the unlikely event that you win?"

"You take your shirt off," Gray replies immediately.

"Seems fair," Kevin agrees with a nod.

"Okay," I say and chalk the end of my cue. "Who's breaking?"

GRAY

She's fucking good.

Bailey circles the pool table, eyeing the balls, gauging where to take her next shot. She's obviously spent many hours at a pool table. I wonder briefly who taught her. Her father? A boyfriend?

"Who taught you to play?" Kevin asks, as if reading my mind.

"My dad's gardener, Mr. Florentine." She smiles softly and takes a shot, missing the hole. "Damn."

"Tell us about him."

"He was old, or so I thought then. I was in my early teens and he was probably in his fifties. My dad had a guesthouse behind our main house that was set up to entertain guests during parties. So it had a pool table and darts and lots of other games, too. I spent a lot of time alone, so Mr. Florentine befriended me and showed me how to play pool."

"Why were you alone?" I ask softly. She'll never be alone again, I can guarantee that.

"Because I had tutors. I wasn't allowed to go to regular school or do things with kids my age. I had housekeepers and other staff in the house, and when I was really little, I had nannies." She laughs and shrugs. "It wasn't so bad."

"It was lonely," Kevin replies before taking his shot and sinking the ball.

"It could be. So I practiced a lot at the pool table." She takes a sip of soda and changes the subject. "Gray tells me that you two were neighbors."

Kevin nods and chalks his que. "Yeah, we were. Our dads still own the houses."

"And your moms?" she asks innocently.

Kevin's head whips up and he stares at me in surprise. "You didn't tell her?" I shake my head no. "Ah, hell."

"Tell me what?"

"My mom passed away when I was ten," I reply softly. "So, it was just my dad and me after that. But Kevin's folks included us in most of their holidays and I was over at their place everyday after school while Dad was still at work."

Bailey walks around the table and wraps her arms around me. "I'm so sorry."

"Oh sweetheart, that was a very long time ago. I'm fine." But I wouldn't have gotten through it as well as I did had it not been for Kev.

"Well, it's new for me so let me feel sorry for you."

I chuckle and kiss her head. "God, you're sweet."

"What about your mama?" Bailey asks Kevin. My heart goes out to him as he looks down at the table and shrugs.

"She passed away about a year ago from cancer."

Bailey kisses my chest, then walks to Kevin to offer the same soothing support.

"I'm sorry."

"I'm okay, princess."

"You've both lost your moms."

We nod and I watch Bailey as she sits on a stool, lost in thought. "You must have really grown to depend on each other through the years."

Kevin catches my eye and raises a brow. "Yeah," he says.

"Hmm." She rubs her finger over her lips, and I want nothing more than to pull her hand away and cover those lips with mine. "Do you think that's why you have the relationship you do?"

"Are you a shrink?" Kevin asks with a laugh, making her blush.

"I don't mean to pry."

"It's probably part of it," I reply honestly. "We haven't really ever sat down and dissected it. It just is."

She nods and then shrugs it off. "Okay."

"And you, my sweet woman," Kevin says just before he sinks the black eight-ball. "Just lost your shirt."

Bailey's mouth drops as she stares at the table, then she purses her lips and props her hands on those sexy as fuck hips of hers.

"Damn it," she mutters.

"A bet's a bet," Kevin says with a wide grin. "Lose the shirt, Bailey."

She glances over to me and I just raise a brow. "You heard him."

"You know," she says as she smiles sassily and lifts the hem of the shirt, but only far enough to see the tops of her thighs. "We could just make it fair and we could all lose our shirts."

"We didn't lose the bet," I remind her and watch as she slowly, so damned slowly, lifts the hem of the shirt. I can see just the edge of her pussy, then finally the small strip of hair she keeps there.

My cock lengthens and tightens as she keeps tugging the shirt up to her breasts.

"Holy fuck," Kevin whispers.

Holy fuck is right.

She finally lifts the shirt over her head and lets it fall to the floor, then clasps her hands at her waistline. "There, it's gone."

SEVEN
BAILEY

"Come here," Kevin says, his face tight and his green eyes on fire as he leans on the pool table.

Why do I suddenly feel like I'm walking into the lion's den?

I keep my eyes on his and walk slowly to him, then stop directly in front of him, not touching him, though my palms are itching to slide under that T-shirt and explore his smooth skin and muscles.

He taps my chin with his finger, tilting my head up, and leans in to kiss me, brushing his soft lips over mine, then settles in to nibble at the corner of my mouth, sending shivers along my scalp and down my spine.

I can't help it, I brace my hands on his hips and lean in, pressing my nakedness against him as he deepens the kiss. His tongue slips into my mouth and explores me lazily, and when I've been thoroughly kissed, he backs away, kisses my forehead and wraps his arms around me, hugging me close.

"I'm naked, you know." I glance over at Gray, whose arms are crossed over his chest as he watches us with heat and humor in his blue eyes.

"I'm aware," Kevin replies as his hands roam up and down my back. "But anticipation is part of the fun."

Gray smirks and I whip my gaze up to Kevin. "Seriously? I have to just walk around naked all day?"

"You lost the bet," Kevin replies and shrugs, like it's not his fault in the least.

"I can't play pool naked," I insist.

"Oh, I think you can," Gray replies softly. "And I think you'll enjoy taunting us with that incredible body of yours while you do."

"Can I have my shirt back if I win?" I ask hopefully.

"No." Gray smiles smugly as he crosses to me, pulls me out of Kevin's embrace and kisses me fast and hard. "No, you can't."

"Damn," I mutter, making them both laugh. But they're right. Playing pool naked, taunting them both, is damn fun.

Finally, after I've lost the third game, I yawn and stow my cue. "I'm done. You guys play, I'll watch."

"Tired?" Gray asks as he tucks my hair behind my ear.

"Lazy," I say with a smile.

"Come here." Gray lifts me and settles on the couch with me in his lap. Kevin joins us and pulls my feet in his lap and begins to knead my arches.

"Oh God that's good." I lean my head on Gray's shoulder and watch Kevin as he loves on my feet. "You guys are forever touching me."

"We like touching you," Gray whispers in my ear, then kisses my temple. "Speaking of that . . ." He's interrupted by my cell phone beeping with an incoming text. He reaches for my phone and passes it to me.

"Damn, it's work," I mutter and begin to tap the screen, responding to my co-chair on an event we're working on for next month. "A venue just fell through."

"On a Sunday?" Kevin asks with a frown.

"You guys aren't the only ones who work 24/7," I reply with a grin. "I usually work every day. Hey, are you guys going to do the Fireman's marathon in April? I'm planning that one too."

"Why are firemen always asked to do things that require us to run or climb?" Kevin asks with a frown.

"Mostly because we spectators hope against hope that you'll take your shirts off," I reply dryly and raise a brow, staring at their shirts, making them laugh.

"Seriously," Gray replies.

"Oh, I'm very serious," I say and finish typing on my phone.

"Why do you do this?" Gray asks quietly as he tightens his arms around me and kisses my cheek. "You said yesterday that you decided not to use your law degree, but why?"

Kevin watches me quietly as he continues to rub my feet, making me melt just a little more.

"My grandma," I sigh and thrum my fingers up and down Gray's arm. "My father's mother was an amazing woman. I spent a lot of time with her as a child. She was also a senator's wife, but she was never idle. She gardened and volunteered her time in schools and organizing charity functions. She used to always tell me, "Bailey, we are blessed people. But there are plenty who aren't as blessed as we are, and there's nothing wrong with spending our time and money making sure we help make their lives just a little better.""

"I like her already," Kevin whispers.

"Oh, you would have loved her." I bite my lip as a wave

of grief swarms me. "She died when I turned fourteen. But from the time I could walk, I was stuck to her hip, following her around, helping. I learned a lot from her about charity and what it is to be generous and passionate about a cause. I also learned how to grow beautiful tomatoes." I grin and bury my face in Gray's neck, take a deep breath and place a sweet kiss under his chin.

"Mom and Dad thought I should make law my career," I continue. "And organizing charity events a hobby. I went to one job interview and knew, as I was sitting there in that stuffy office, that it wasn't for me. I want to help people, not sue them."

"So you pissed your parents off," Gray guesses correctly.

"Oh, big time," I agree. "Dad yelled and carried on and Mom cried delicately in her two-hundred-dollar handkerchief and both of them glared at me with disappointment and regret. But you know what?" I back away and look Gray right in the eye. "I didn't give a shit. I don't care that I make peanuts and I work long hours. When I hand a check over to an organization that desperately needs the money, it's the best feeling in the world."

"I'm so fucking proud of you," Gray whispers and plants his lips on my forehead.

"You're amazing, princess," Kevin says and rubs his hands up and down my bare legs, then lifts one leg to kiss my knee softly.

"What about you guys? Why firefighting?" I reach over and twine my fingers with Kevin's, then pull his hand up to my lips and press it to my cheek. I love touching my men, even if it is only for one more day that I have unlimited access to them.

"He's a pyromaniac," Kevin says, pointing at Gray.

"Whatever, dude," Gray replies with a roll of the eyes. "This idiot decided he wanted to play with fire and I decided I'd better go with him and make sure he doesn't get himself killed."

"It's dangerous," I say seriously. "Have you ever been hurt?"

They look at each other and then nod thoughtfully.

"It can be dangerous," Kevin says carefully. "But we're trained well and we have a great team."

"Why do I think you just downplayed it?" I ask with a laugh.

"He told you the truth," Gray says with a shrug. "It can be tricky. But we're very careful."

Jesus, what would I do if I lost one of them? And where the fuck did that thought come from? They aren't *mine*. We're just having a fun weekend.

"Can we watch a movie and veg out for a while?" I ask.

"Absolutely," Gray says and kisses my nose, then stands with me still in his arms—Dear sweet Moses, the man is strong—and lowers me to Kevin's lap. "Wanna watch *Backdraft*?"

"No!" I respond immediately. "No firefighter movies. It'll only make me worry more."

"Aww, you worry?" Kevin asks and nuzzles my ear. "That's so sweet."

"Stop it." I giggle when he tickles my side, then sigh when he slips those hands down my side to my lower belly.

"Okay, what do you want to watch?"

"Something with action and hot shirtless men, since my hot men won't get shirtless for me." I pout my lip out, but Kevin kisses me sweetly, making me melt against him. "God, you're good at the kissing thing."

"You like being kissed," he whispers.

"Yeah."

"Good 'cause we like kissing you."

I smile up at him and drag my fingers down his cheek.

"Hello? Focus here," Gray says. "Movie."

We finally agree on something with lots of car chases and guns shooting and settle in to watch it. I slide my ass onto the cushion between the guys, my torso leaning on Kevin and legs over Gray's lap. It feels . . . *right*. Like I'm supposed to be right here, between them, always.

This has been the best weekend of my life. These men are loving and affectionate, and I'll be the first to admit that's something that I've lacked in my twenty-seven years, so it's no wonder that I've soaked it up and fallen hopelessly in love with them.

With both of them.

They each bring so much to the table. Gray is quiet and intense, while Kevin is more outgoing and quick-witted. They're both sexy as hell and have so much love to give.

How could I ever choose between them? It's insane to think that we could go on having a relationship between the three of us. Life doesn't work like that. At some point I'll have to choose, or ask them to, and that's not fair.

Not to anyone.

I bite my lip and keep my eyes trained on the TV as Mark Wahlburg and Charlize Theron try to break into a safe, but I'm not paying attention to the movie.

This is my last few hours with them. I have to go back to my apartment tonight and back to my regularly scheduled life tomorrow. And the thought of it makes me ridiculously sad.

Maybe I should go now, rather than prolong it, like ripping off a Band-Aid.

My mind made up, I stand and walk toward the stairs.

"Do you want us to pause it, sweetheart?" Gray asks.

"No, thanks." I shake my head, but don't look back. If I look back I'll climb back on that couch with them and beg them to let me stay. I've quickly become addicted to their touch, to their sweet words.

I need to go home.

I hurry up to the master bedroom and stuff my dirty clothes into my bag, pull on a shirt and pants and sweep my toiletries into my bag as well. I tidy the room as best as I can and trudge back down to the basement, my bag and purse slung over my shoulder.

The guys are still watching the movie intently. Kevin glances up as I walk into his line of vision, then does a double take.

"What the fuck?" he demands, as he and Gray stand and glare at my bag.

"Can someone please take me home now?" I ask, hating that my voice sounds weak and shaky.

"Where are you going, sweetheart?" Gray asks. Kevin's jaw clenches as he crosses his arms over his chest.

"I think I should just go ahead and go home. I have an early morning tomorrow, and I have some things to do." I shrug and bite my lip. *I will not cry.*

"Did we do something wrong?" Kevin asks.

"What? No, of course not." I shake my head adamantly. "I've had a great weekend with both of you. Thank you for everything. Maybe we can do it again sometime." I smile bravely and then frown in confusion when Kevin growls and Gray shoves his hand through his hair in frustration.

"You're not leaving," Kevin says, his voice matter of fact.

"Excuse me?"

"You heard him."

EIGHT
GRAY

Her eyebrows rise in surprise and she licks her delicious lips as she blinks twice, looking back and forth between us.

"Planning to kidnap me?" she asks and crosses her arms over her chest.

"We're fucking this up," I mutter and pace away as I drag my hand roughly over my face.

"No, of course not," Kevin replies. "We were planning to talk to you about you staying. Here. With us."

"Why?" she asks, surprised.

"Well, for one, because your apartment isn't safe," Kevin replies and I cringe as I turn to see Bailey narrow her eyes on my soon-to-be dead friend.

"My apartment," she replies with ice dripping off her voice, "is perfectly fine. I'm a grown woman, and I don't belong to anyone, so where I decide to live isn't anyone's business."

"That's where you're wrong," I reply quietly. I can't look away from her. God, she's so beautiful. "You do belong to someone. You belong to us."

She closes her eyes and her lip quivers, and I'm suddenly terrified of two things: One, that she's going to cry. God, please don't cry. And two, that she just might not want us back.

"This is crazy," she whispers. "For how long, Gray?"

"What do you mean?"

"The threesome thing is fun, don't get me wrong, but for how long can it go on?"

Kevin and I share a confused glance, then look back to Bailey.

"For as long as the three of us want it to, sweetheart."

She paces away, staring at the pool table for a long minute, then turns back to us.

"When we first met, I had no idea you would both be so important to me. I love you both so much and it confuses the hell out of me. Eventually I'll have to choose, and I can't do that."

She loves us!

"No, baby, you don't have to choose," Kevin says and steps toward her, but she holds a hand up, stopping him.

"People don't live their lives in threesomes, they do it in pairs. I know this is new, and it's fun, but it's turned into more than just a sexy good time for me, and I know that I would rather die than have to choose between you. It would break my heart."

She firms her chin and keeps her tears at bay, and I swear I've never loved anyone the way I love her right now.

"I love you too," I whisper.

"And *I* love you as well, princess."

"Oh God." She covers her mouth with her hand and shakes her head. "I knew someone would get hurt."

"If you'd listen to fucking reason, no one would get hurt," Kevin says with frustration.

"Have we said anything about choosing?" I ask her calmly. She's admitted that she loves us. The rest is just details.

"No," she says. "And I love that you're not jealous of each other . . ."

"I'm not done," I interrupt. "What did I say to you the other night?"

"That what happens between the three of us is just between the three of us."

"I didn't mean that just for this weekend, sweetheart." I step forward and take her shoulders in my hands.

"And that's great in theory, but . . ."

"Love doesn't have to be perfect," Kevin says. "It just has to be real."

"We want you to stay," I repeat.

"Until I get a better apartment?" she says with a quiver in her voice.

"Fuck that apartment, or any other apartment. You have a home here."

Her eyes widen and she glances from me to Kevin, who's come up beside us. He tucks her hair behind her ear and kisses her forehead.

"You want me to move in with you? *Permanently?*"

We both nod and watch her carefully as her shoulders sag.

"Stay," Kevin whispers.

"It's really too soon," she says without conviction. Kevin laughs and nudges my shoulder.

"I told you she'd say that."

"You've talked about this?" she asks.

"Yes," I reply. "We both love you and already consider you ours."

She sighs and offers us each a small smile. "What now?"

"Now," Kevin says as he lifts her, wrapping her legs around his hips. "We make love to you in *our* bed."

KEVIN

She weighs nothing in my arms as I lay her in the middle of our bed. Yet she's *everything* we've ever wanted, in every way.

"Are you both sure?" she asks, holding my face in her small hands and gazing into my eyes.

"We've never been more sure," I assure her and kiss her lips softly as I roll to her side. Gray sweeps up onto her other side and brushes her hair aside so he can press kisses to her neck, making her squirm.

"Remember that first time with the two of us?" Gray asks in her ear. She shivers, making me grin.

"How can I forget that?" she says with a laugh.

"We don't ever have to go farther than that, sweetheart," he says.

She frowns up at me in confusion, then her eyes light up when she realizes what he's talking about. "I've had anal sex before, but this is very new to me."

I'll kill him. Whoever he is.

Gray and I share a heated glance. I take a deep breath and calm my irrational temper.

"Did you like it?" I ask her.

"Not really." She wrinkles her adorable nose. "It wasn't fantastic. But . . ." She bites her lip.

"But?" I whisper and kiss her lips softly as Gray goes to work undressing her.

"But it would be amazing to feel you both at the same time."

It's a whispered admission, and honestly surprises me.

"It's something Gray and I have only done a handful of times, Bailey. It's never felt right for us either. But I have a feeling this will be different."

"What's different about me?" she asks with a frown.

"Everything," we reply in unison.

"It's about trust," Gray says softly and kisses her shoulder. He's tweaking her nipple between his fingers. "And respect." Kiss. "Affection."

"Love," I whisper as I slide my hand down her flat belly to her sweet spot. "God, you're so wet, princess."

"I've been wet all damn day," she replies with a smile. "You two pack quite a punch."

I grin wolfishly and kiss her hard as Gray rolls over to his back.

"Come here, sweetheart." He guides her up to her knees and turns her to face his feet and positions her pussy over his face.

The lucky motherfucker.

GRAY

She braces her hands on my chest and gently lowers her pussy to my face. "God, she smells un-fucking-believable," I growl and take a deep breath. Her lips are shiny from the juices from her pussy and her clit is already poking out from under its hood.

I part her lips and drag my fingertip through the folds, wetting it, then slide it over her clit and back down again.

"Oh God, Gray," she moans and circles her hips above me. I fucking love the sound of my name on her lips.

"Feel good?" I ask before pulling her down closer so I can wrap my lips around her labia and push my tongue inside her.

We have to get her good and turned on so we don't hurt her.

Suddenly, I hear sucking sounds and Kevin moan long and low and I know that Bailey is sucking him.

Lucky motherfucker.

This woman can suck the hell out of a cock. I feel my own dick lengthen and harden as I lap at her juices. She tastes like honey. I'll never get enough of her.

She grinds down against me harder, rubbing her clit against my chin as I fuck her with my tongue. I can feel the contractions begin and I know she's about to come.

"Let her go over, man," Kevin says just as she cries out and comes violently on my face. It's fucking awesome.

Suddenly, she takes my cock in her hand and begins jacking me as Kevin moves away from her and guides her down to suck me before moving behind her.

How the fuck is a man supposed to concentrate on eating pussy when she's sucking his cock like a champ?

Having her leaning over me has opened her up nicely for Kevin. I lift her off my face so he can sink his fingers in her and coat them with her wetness, then guide her back down to me as he circles the rim of her tight hole with his fingertip.

"Oh God," she cries.

BAILEY

"Shh, baby," Kevin croons as he rubs his big hand up and down my back soothingly. He's teasing my ass, as Gray licks and sucks my pussy. The combined sensations are off the chart, sending tingles through my entire body.

I return to sucking Gray's cock, pushing him to the back of my throat so I can swallow around the head. He grips my hips desperately, and I know I'm making him crazy.

I love making him crazy.

"You're so beautiful, princess," Kevin murmurs and kisses my lower back. "You have such a gorgeous little ass."

I can hear a cap open, then close, and his finger is back, massaging me firmly and then his finger is suddenly inside me.

"Oh God!"

"Is this okay, baby?" Kevin asks. "God, you're tight."

I nod as I suck Gray, moaning and circling my hips. God, I can't stop grinding on his magical mouth. The pressure is building again but before I can come, Gray lifts me off his mouth and scoots out from under me.

"Where are you going?" I demand. "I was about to come!"

"I know," he replies with a laugh. "We need to keep you just on the edge for a few more minutes."

"That's just mean."

"No, baby." He wipes his face off before kissing me long and deep. Kevin is still behind me, his finger in me, and it's surprisingly . . . *hot*.

"It'll go easier on you the more turned on you are," Kevin says against my shoulder as he kisses me there.

"I'm so fucking turned on," I reply and cup Gray's face in my hand. "Please."

"What do you need?"

"You!"

Gray grins before lying down again. Kevin has to pull out

of me as Gray guides me over him, straddling his hips.

"Kevin's going to take your ass for the first time, sweetheart," he says as he guides his hard cock inside me and pulls my hips down until I'm completely impaled on him.

"Why?" I ask breathlessly.

"I'm man enough to admit that I'm a bit smaller than him," Kevin says from beside me. He's kneading my ass cheek and leans in to pull my nipple in his mouth.

"There's nothing *small* about either of you," I reply truthfully. Kevin smiles and kisses me hard, cradling my face in his hands as Gray begins to move in and out of me, making me moan.

"I love you for that, princess. But I'm a bit thinner." He grins. "And this is a contest I don't mind losing when you're the prize."

"Are you okay?" Gray asks me as he pulls me down against him and takes my lips with his.

"Mm," I reply. I sink my fingers in his thick black hair, rest my elbows on the bed beside his head and settle in to kiss him for about a year.

"Still sure?" Gray whispers against my lips.

"It's about trust and respect, right?" I whisper back.

"And love," Kevin reminds me as he covers me from behind and kisses my shoulder.

"Then yeah, I'm sure."

"All you have to say is *stop*, and it'll stop," Kevin insists. "We promise."

"I know." I nod and smile down into bright blue eyes as Kevin inserts a finger once more. Now I'm full of Gray, and the feel of just that finger makes me sigh in pleasure. "Holy shit," I breathe.

Gray's breath is coming faster now as he watches me closely.

I know that at the first sign of distress he'll put an end to it, but God it feels amazing.

"I'm sliding in another finger, baby," Kevin says as he continues to kiss my back. He's panting now too, and the wait has to be killing him. He adds a finger and stills for a few moments, then begins to work his fingers in wide circles.

"Fuuuuck," I moan as I ride Gray, clenching around him. "Oh God, guys."

"Tell me before you come," Kevin instructs me. Gray cups my face and kisses me hard.

"How do you feel?" he breathes.

"Amazing," I reply with a smile.

"Oh, you're definitely fucking amazing," he says.

"I think I'm gonna . . ."

Before I can complete the sentence, Kevin pulls his fingers out and quickly replaces them with his cock, nudging the head inside and then slides all the way in and covers both Gray and I with his large body.

"Fuck!" Gray cries and I bite my lip at the sting of tears.

"Are you okay," Kevin asks me urgently. "Talk to me, Bailey."

"So good," I choke out. And it is. Holy shit, it *so* is. I feel full to bursting, but feeling them both inside me at once is *life changing*. "Oh God, so good."

"I'm not going to move yet," Kevin says through clenched teeth. "Just get used to us."

Gray and Kevin lock gazes over my shoulder as they each take one of my hands and link our fingers.

We're connected, in the most miraculous way I've ever experienced.

"You can move," I whisper and gasp when Kevin pulls out,

and as he pushes back in, Gray pulls out, relieving the full sensation, but making my body explode in electricity. They set a smooth rhythm, a push-pull, that makes me tingle, and makes me feel like the most desirable woman they've ever known. Their free hands are *everywhere*. On my back, my breasts, my hips as they rock their bodies in tandem.

"Can you feel each other?" I whisper.

"Oh yeah," Gray says with a grin. "I can feel him."

"Does it bother you?"

"Fuck no," Kevin says as he bites gently on my shoulder. "It doesn't bother us, princess."

"Do you know how incredible you both are?" I ask.

"Oh God, I'm not going to last," Kevin gasps as I feel him shiver and explode inside me just as Gray bites his lip and pushes deep inside me, tipping me over the edge with them, coming long and hard, my body wracked in contractions.

It's the most intense orgasm of my life.

When we've all regained our senses, the guys pull out of me and roll me onto my side.

"Are you okay?" Kevin asks as he brushes my hair off my cheeks and kisses me tenderly on my lips, then my cheek.

"I can't imagine feeling much better than this," I reply with a smile.

Gray is nuzzling my breasts, gently kissing my nipples, then drags his nose up my neck and kisses me softly.

"I love you, sweetheart."

"I love you," I reply happily. I reach for Kevin's hand and kiss it, then look up into his amazing green eyes. "And I love you."

NINE
KEVIN

Three months later . . .

"Where is she?" I ask as I pace the floor and glance out the living room window for the third time.

"You've asked me that six times in the past five minutes. She's on her way," Gray replies calmly and shakes his head at me.

"How can you be so calm?"

"Getting all worked up isn't going to get her here any sooner."

"I hate it when you're rational." I glare at him.

"I'm surprised you know the meaning of the word," he replies with a laugh and only laughs harder when I flip him off. "Is that any way to treat me on a day like today?"

I shove my hand through my hair and pace away, glancing around our house. Bailey has added so much to our home. She's decorated and added plants and fussy touches here and there. But more than that, she's made us come alive.

She's the best part of us.

Now, if she would just get her sexy ass home . . .

GRAY

I'm as keyed up as Kevin is. Where the fuck is she? She called us from her event site forty-five minutes ago and said she was on her way home. She should have been here twenty minutes ago.

"Maybe she got stuck in traffic," Kevin suggests.

"It's a bit late in the evening for traffic," I remind him, making him growl.

"She's doing this on purpose. She knows and she's doing it on purpose."

"She doesn't know a thing about it," I reply, sounding much calmer than I feel. *Shit, could she know?*

"Did you get the back yard set up?" he asks anxiously.

"You know I did. You just saw it yourself." I shake my head in exasperation. "Jesus, calm the fuck down."

"What if she's been *in* an accident?" he asks, near hysteria when we both hear her car door slam and whip toward the front door.

She walks in with a small smile on her lips and when she looks up at us that smile blooms across her face, lighting her up.

God, every time I look at her it's as if it's the first time.

BAILEY

"When you smile at me like that, it's like a kick to the gut," Kevin whispers and Gray nods beside him. They're both staring at me like they're starving tigers and I'm dinner.

I fucking love it when they look at me like this. It usually means we're about to have a damn fun time.

"Hey, guys." I tilt my head as I shut the door behind me. "What's going on?"

"Why does anything have to be going on?" Gray asks. "Can't we just be happy to see you?"

I drop my bags on the nearest couch and prop my hands on my hips as I watch them.

"I love it that you're happy to see me but you both look guilty. What's going on?"

They glance at each other and then laugh as they each take a hand and kiss it, then take turns kissing my lips quickly.

Way too quickly.

"Kissing is always good," I murmur and lean in for another, but Gray chuckles and kisses my forehead instead.

"And you'll get plenty, but first we want to show you something."

"Ah, the plot thickens."

They flank me, looping my arms through theirs, and escort me through the house to the back patio.

"Oh, wow," I whisper as I take in the white lights that have been strung over head and the table covered in a huge bouquet of my favorite stargazer lilies.

"Here." Kevin pulls a chair back from the table and motions for me to sit in it. As I do, both men take one knee before me. I cover my mouth with both hands and watch them through tear-filled eyes.

"Are you kidding me?" I whisper.

Gray smiles in that sweet way he does when I've amused him and Kevin just chuckles and shakes his head.

"Can we have your hands, please?" Gray asks.

They each take a ring box out of their pockets.

"We had trouble deciding who should go first, but finally came to the conclusion that we should do it based on who's oldest, so I get to go first," Kevin says with a wink.

"You're two months older." I laugh and dab at my eyes with a napkin, then give them my hands again.

"He's still older," Gray replies with a laugh.

"And nervous," Kevin adds as he licks his lips. Oh, my sweet man. He's good at being silly and outspoken, but I've learned that he has a soft side too. "I love you, Bailey." He pins me in his green gaze. His blonde hair is all messed up from his nervous fingers, I'm sure. "You've brought so much to my life in the past few months. I can't imagine my life without you, and I don't ever want to know what that reality feels like. I want you to be mine, to be *ours* for the rest of our lives."

Gray clears his throat, catching my attention. His blue eyes are calm and clear. "I love you Bailey, for all of the million little things that make you you, and for all of the ways you've made us better. I can't wait to see what the future brings for us."

They glance at each other and then back at me as the tears finally spill over and down my cheeks.

"Marry us," Gray says. "Spend the rest of your life with us."

"We will spend every day of our lives devoted to you, Bailey. We promise you that."

I bring their hands up to my lips and kiss them both at the same time.

"I would be honored to marry you," I reply and find myself in the biggest bear hug of my life, trapped between two very strong, very happy men. Gray lifts me off my feet and kisses me with everything he has, then passes me off to Kevin for the same treatment before they open the ring boxes, which are both . . . *empty.*

"That's the way to knock a girl off her feet," I say with a laugh. *What do my amazing men have up their sleeves?*

"We thought of each buying you a knockout engagement ring, and you could wear one on each hand," Gray begins.

"Then we thought about buying just one ring," Kevin continues. They're both looking down at the boxes, almost as if they're embarrassed, then they both look up at me.

"But that's not who you are," Gray says. "Every time we try to spoil you with something expensive, you decline."

"I don't need . . ." I begin but Kevin lays his finger over my lips, shutting me up.

"Yes, we've heard it, over and over again," he says with a smile.

"We'd like for us to all wear matching platinum bands, if that's okay with you," Gray says. "If we're way off base here and you'd rather have the diamonds, we'll happily buy them, but we didn't think that's what you'd want."

God, they know me so well. I swipe at the tears pouring down my cheeks and shake my head.

"Oh shit, we fucked up." Kevin rubs his fingers over his lips as I laugh.

"No, you're right. This is perfect. Matching bands are perfect." I pull both of their faces close and kiss them, then they lean their foreheads against mine. "I love you both so much. How do we do this? I'm quite sure a marriage between the three of us isn't legal, even in the state of Washington."

"No," Kevin agrees and looks at Gray.

"You'll marry Kevin legally and take his name," Gray says

and shushes me as I begin to protest. "He's the oldest."

"We come to the table equally, Bailey," Kevin continues. "We make the same amount of money, and most of what we own is in both our names. Either of us can put you on our insurance policies. We can both take care of you equally, so we decided that it should be the older of the two of us."

I shake my head and bite my lips. "It doesn't feel right."

"Washington is a liberal state, sweetheart, but not that liberal." Gray smiles and brushes his knuckles down my cheek. "It's okay. *We* know that we love each other and are committed to each other."

I chew on my lip, considering the options. "I'll legally marry Kevin, but I'm changing my name to Bailey Welling-McDermitt."

Both of their jaws drop as they watch me in a stunned silence.

"You'd do that?" Gray's voice is hoarse as his eyes fill with tears.

"People will know, Bailey. You won't be able to hide that you're married to both of us." Kevin tucks my hair behind my ear. "Are you sure you want that?"

"Are you ashamed of me?" I ask uncertainly. "Are you ashamed of the three of us being together?"

"Hell no," they reply in unison.

"Fuck people then," I insist. "You will be my husbands. I'm not ashamed of either of you. I *love* you." I link my fingers with theirs again. "If we're going to do this thing, we're going to do it right. I'll take both of your names."

"I love you so much," Gray whispers and he crushes me against him, clinging to me.

"I love you too."

"Well," Kevin says and he kisses my forehead and wipes the tears from my cheek and Gray continues to hold me against him. "It's going to be one hell of an adventure."

"My favorite kind," I reply with a wide smile.

The End

52370957R00050

Made in the USA
Columbia, SC
02 March 2019